# Max's Mask

## A PURIM STORY

Havvah Deevon

ILLUSTRATIONS BY
Itay Bekin

Kalaniot Books
Moosic, Pennsylvania

**This is Max.** Starting at a new school can be hard, but Max really likes Miss Tzipi's classroom. Miss Tzipi knows just how a superhero feels.

Max loves the blocks in his new kindergarten class. He has blocks at home, but the blocks at school are so big they can almost reach the ceiling!

But sometimes David knocks them down.

Max also has fun lining up all the cars in a row. They start at the bookshelf and go all the way around the corner—almost the entire length of the classroom!

But sometimes David kicks them over.
Miss Tzipi comes by to help. "Can you boys work together to clean this up?"

One day Miss Tzipi asks the class, "Can anyone tell me what holiday is coming soon? Don't forget to raise your hand."

Caleb raises his hand. "It's Purim, the holiday when brave Queen Esther saves the day and we dress up in costumes! I'm going to be an astronaut."

Rachel raises her hand and says that she will be a princess or Queen Esther. Becky jumps up and says, "I want to be Queen Esther too!"

David raises his hand and says, "My costume is a secret."

Ruth says, "I will dress up as Albert Einstein."

"Interesting!" says Miss Tzipi. "Can anyone tell the others who Albert Einstein was?"

Max quickly replies, "He was a scientist." He almost forgets that he is supposed to raise his hand.

David sticks his tongue out at Max.

The next day Miss Tzipi tells the children the story of Purim. "A long, long time ago in a kingdom called Persia, King Ahasuerus was looking for a new queen. He sent his men all over his vast kingdom, north and south, east and west, to find the most beautiful girl in the kingdom. And of all the girls, Esther was chosen because she was so very beautiful. But what the king didn't realize was that she was also brave, wise—and Jewish.

"Esther had a cousin, Mordecai, who learned that the king's evil adviser Haman wanted to harm the Jews. Mordecai asked Esther to help. Bravely, Esther finally told the king that she was Jewish and that Haman's evil plan would hurt her and her people. The king, moved by Esther's plea and impressed by her courage in speaking out, put an end to evil Haman's plot. Esther's courage saved the Jews!

"At Purim we celebrate Esther's and Mordecai's bravery and wisdom. And we hide our true selves until we choose not to, just like Esther did. This is why we wear costumes on Purim."

Then Miss Tzipi sends the kids to the dress-up corner to look for a costume for the big Purim party tomorrow.

Max finds a crown. *Maybe I will be powerful King Ahasuerus for Purim*, he thinks.

But David wants the crown too. He tries to grab it.
Max does not let go. He found it first.

Max continues to think about his costume. He thinks about it while he is at the supermarket with Dad.

He thinks about it while he is in the bath.
He thinks about it after his bath.

Mom suggests that Max dress as a lion. Dad suggests an astronaut. Max says that Caleb is already dressing as an astronaut.

"Well," says Dad, "it is possible that several children will dress up in the same costume. That's okay."

Indeed, Rachel, Becky, Nilli, Leah, Amelia, and Dalia all dress as Queen Esther! They all stand together. Their parents take pictures and applaud.

Ariel dresses as an artist,

Daniel and Eliana dress as firefighters,

Noah and Naomi dress as laboratory researchers, and Niko and Hannah dress as police officers.

There are all kinds of costumes. "Everyone who dressed up as an astronaut, please step forward," says Miss Tzipi. Two astronauts stand in front of the parents. Everyone claps and takes pictures.

"Albert Einstein, please stand up," announces Miss Tzipi. Ruth's mother claps, and her baby brother waves a flag.

After a bit, Miss Tzipi looks around and asks, "Did we forget anyone? Max what about you?"

Max thinks to himself, *I don't need a costume anymore.* So he just shakes his head and smiles at Miss Tzipi.

After the parents go home, the children play. Max starts to build a car. An astronaut comes to help Max search for the right pieces. "You search and I will build, okay?" Max suggests.

The astronaut digs into the box and hands Max a piece. "This is great!" says Max. They continue to work together until they build a cool car.

"Phew! I am hot," says the astronaut and removes his helmet.

"You are David!" exclaims Max.
"Yes," says David, "It's me."
And Max says, "I'm Max."

# About This Story

The holiday of Purim celebrates the Jewish people's narrow escape from harm during the fifth century BCE in Persia. This vast kingdom stretched from what is modern-day Iran to India in the Far East and to Cush, the ancient kingdom of Ethiopia, in the West. As told in the Bible, King Ahasuerus holds a banquet for the men in Shushan, the country's capital. Vashti, his current queen, holds another event for the women. Ahasuerus asks Vashti to dance at his event, and she refuses. This angers the king, and he decides to choose a new queen. He sends his counselors all over the kingdom to help him select a new queen. Out of all the millions of women in this huge kingdom (and against her will), a young Jewish girl named Esther is chosen. As it happens, Esther's cousin Mordecai is a member of the king's court. Mordecai is surprised that Esther is chosen, and as a measure of caution, he suggests she keep her Jewish background a secret.

Meanwhile, Haman, an adviser to the king, is becoming more and more powerful, so powerful that he insists that everyone bow down to him. Mordecai refuses, because as a Jew he bows down only to God. Haman is furious. When he learns that Mordecai is Jewish, he plots to kill not only him, but all the Jews. Mordecai tells Esther of Haman's plan and asks that she convince the king to stop Haman. Though frightened for her life, Esther reveals her Jewish identity to the king. She tells him of Haman's plan to kill the Jews and explains that this would mean death to her as well. Moved by his queen's bravery, the king puts an end to this plan, and the Jews are saved. Esther and Mordecai recorded this story and sent it all over the Persian kingdom to every Jewish community. Today, we celebrate Purim during the Hebrew month of Adar in the spring. We read the Scroll of Esther, and every time the name of Haman is spoken, we make loud sounds by yelling or using a noisemaker called a grogger, so his name and legacy are drowned out. We give gifts of food called *mishloach manot* to friends and family and charity to those in need. And just as Queen Esther hid her identity as a Jew, we hide who we are by wearing a costume.

In this book, Max also wears a costume. He is new to Miss Tzipi's classroom, and he is nervous. The toys are different from his toys at home. His classmates are new to him as well. He has never met someone like David. Wearing a superhero costume is a way for Max to deal with some of these big emotions. After all, as a superhero, he will have superpowers! However, as Max begins to realize his own character and strengths, he is better able to interact with these new classmates—even David. Ultimately, he sees that he has his own superpowers and doesn't need a costume. Max can simply be . . . Max.

To all the real superheroes:
those who struggle, but ultimately overcome their fears.
—H. D.

*All Kalaniot Books have accompanying activity guides.*
*Download them for free at KalaniotBooks.com.*

Text copyright © 2024 by Havvah Deevon
Illustrations copyright © 2024 by Itay Bekin
Published in Hebrew by Kinneret-Zmora-Dvir
This English language edition published in 2025 by Kalaniot Books,
an imprint of Endless Mountains Publishing Company
72 Glenmaura National Boulevard, Suite 104B, Moosic, Pennsylvania 18507
www.KalaniotBooks.com
All rights reserved. No part of this book may be reproduced, stored in a retrieval system,
or transmitted in any form or by any means—electronic, mechanical, photocopying, recording,
or otherwise—without the prior written permission of Endless Mountains Publishing Company,
except for the inclusion of brief quotations in an acknowledged review.
Library of Congress Control Number: 2024944525
ISBN: 978-1-962011-02-0
Printed in China
First Printing